HABITATS OF *THE WORLD*

MOUNTAINS

Written and Illustrated by
Sheri Amsel

A LUCAS • EVANS BOOK

RSVP
RAINTREE STECK-VAUGHN
PUBLISHERS
The Steck-Vaughn Company
Austin, Texas

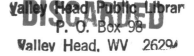

For my husband Richard

Consultant: James G. Doherty, General Curator, Bronx Zoo, Bronx, New York

Book Design: M 'N O Production Services, Inc.

Library of Congress Cataloging-in-Publication Data

Amsel, Sheri.
    Mountains / written and illustrated by Sheri Amsel.
        p.   cm. —— (Habitats of the world)
    "A Lucas/Evans book."
    Includes index.
    Summary: Discusses the plant and animal life of the world's mountains and the need to conserve mountain habitats.
    ISBN 0-8114 6303-6 (lib. bdg.)   ISBN 0-8114-4922-X (softcover)
    1. Alpine fauna—Habitat—Juvenile literature.   2. Alpine flora—Habitat—Juvenile literature.
3. Mountain ecology—Juvenile literature.   4. Mountains—Juvenile literature.
[1. Alpine animals.   2. Alpine plants.   3. Mountains.]
    I. Title.   II. Series: Amsel, Sheri. Habitats of the world.
    QH87.A57   1993
    574.5'264—dc20   92-8791
                                                                                       CIP
                                                                                       AC

Printed and bound in the United States.

3 4 5 6 7 8 9 0 VH 98 97 96 95 94

Table of Contents

		page
1.	Mountains of the World	4
2.	The Rocky Mountains	6
3.	The Andes	14
4.	The Alps	19
5.	The Himalayas	23
6.	Mountains Today	29
7.	Glossary	30
8.	Index	31

MOUNTAINS OF THE WORLD

When you think of climbing a mountain, do you think of roping up a snow-covered peak in the Himalayas with a team or scrambling up alone through rocks and fragile alpine plants in the Rocky Mountains? Both are considered mountains but are distinctly different.

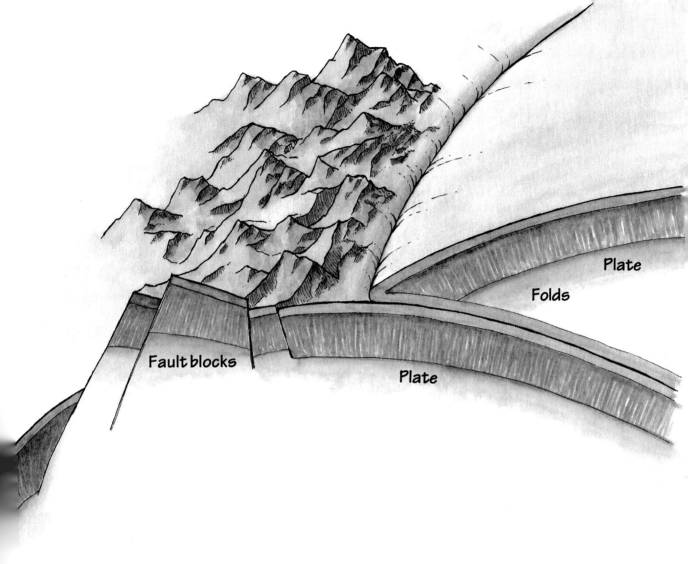

Plate

Folds

Fault blocks

Plate

Mountains are formed by movements of the earth's crust, made up of drifting plates. When the plates collide, over millions of years, they heave up into faults and folds, forming mountain ranges. Volcanoes, such as those crowning much of the Andes Mountains, also push up through the earth's crust. Fault blocks rise up to become jagged peaks, and folds form more round peaks.

Though we'll look at only a few mountain ranges, mountains all over the world have various shapes and formations and have a great variety of life on them.

The Rocky Mountains

The Rocky Mountains stretch 3,000 miles like a jagged backbone down the western United States and Canada. They form the continental divide. This term means that the river systems on one side of the continent flow toward the east, and on the other side they flow toward the west.

Cougar

Snowshoe hare

Forested slopes lead up to sparse rock summits here, and are the home of the lynx, bobcat, and cougar. The big cats hunt deer, snowshoe hare, mice, and grouse. Seeing a cougar in the wild was, for many years, a rare and amazing sight, due to its being overhunted and to its shy nature. But in the beginning of the 1990s whitetail deer numbers were very high, and with the abundance of this food, the cougar numbers rose dramatically.

Grizzly bears still roam in the Montana and Canadian Rockies. But like the cougar, they need large tracts of wilderness on which to hunt and breed. The numbers of grizzlies decline as roads and development push through the northern Rockies.

Grizzly bear

Herds of bison and elk are a familiar sight in Yellowstone National Park. Unlike the great herds of bison that made the ground tremble with their passage, the Yellowstone bison herds are kept down to a number that will not overgraze the park's grasslands and foothills.

Elk

Bison

Maple

Mule deer

Chokecherry

Alder

Ruffed grouse

On the lower slopes, maple, chokecherry, alder, and water birch provide forage for groups of mule deer. Higher up on the mountains, Engelmann spruce, western larch, and ponderosa pine take over. Ruffed grouse blend into the underbrush.

Weasel, mink, and pine marten are among the smaller predators. Hunting for birds, mice, eggs, or insects, they move quickly through the rocks and trees.

Coyotes travel in pairs, families, or alone looking for winter-killed animals or leftovers from a cougar or grizzly kill.

Pine marten

Coyote

Weasel

Bald eagle

Bighorn
sheep

Mountain
goat

Marmot

Up higher among the rocks, marmots forage for short alpine grasses.
Mountain goats and herds of bighorn sheep defy steep cliffs as they
leap from rock to rock. Bald eagles keep a watchful eye for small or
dead animals to bring back to their nesting young.

The eastern slopes of the Rockies are arid, with fewer trees and a sandy grassland feeling. Here and on the high alpine meadows, wild-flowers bring brilliant color to the warmer seasons of the Rockies. Indian paintbrushes, bitterroot, lupine, and balsamroot cover the hills. Wild geranium lure elk, deer, and even bears out of the forest to graze. Bear grass sends its tall white shoots into the air.

People come to the Rockies to see the diverse life and experience the wilderness. As a way of preserving these areas for everyone to enjoy, the national parks were formed. The abundance of wildlife and breathtaking views have actually drawn too many people to these parks. Now, to keep a habitat natural, human traffic has to be limited.

Elk

Indian paintbrush

Wild geranium

Lupine

Bear grass

Bitterroot

Balsamroot

The Andes

The Andes are the longest chain of mountains in the world. They stretch along the entire west coast of South America from Panama to Cape Horn on the southern tip of the continent. The highest peak is 22,000 feet, and the many ranges or "cordillas" of mountains that make up the Andes form a barrier of continuous rock and snow for 5,000 miles.

The Andes were formed millions of years ago by folds and faults in the earth's crust. Weird, jagged shapes were cut and left by ancient, shifting glaciers. Volcanoes have pushed up through many of the mountains. The Andes include deep gorges in green tropical mountains and high, jagged snowcapped peaks. Many of the high peaks are still covered by glacial ice. Because the Andes run north and south and because they vary in elevation, the vegetation found from place to place can differ greatly.

15

On high plateaus, vicunas run wild in small herds, grazing on the sparse grass. They are a high-altitude animal, living at 12,000 feet and protected from the fierce cold by their thick, woolly fleeces. Another Andean animal famous for its beautiful hide is the little chinchilla. Both the chinchilla and the vicuna have been heavily hunted by humans for their silken fur. The chinchillas were so overhunted that now they survive only in the high Chilean Andes. Living in groups, they burrow in the rocky slopes, feeding at night and relaxing in the warm morning sun.

Chinchilla

Vicuna

Darwin's rhea, an ostrich-like bird also shares the high plateaus, grazing and traveling in small groups. The Andean condor, biggest of all vultures, glides on a 10-foot wingspan searching for small prey or carrion. Bright red cock-in-the-rocks nest on high cliffs overlooking river gorges. Animals here have to adapt to strong winds that blow all the time in these rugged mountains.

Andean condor

Cock-of-the-rock

Darwin's rhea

The Alps

The largest mountain range in Europe, the Alps, forms an impressive border between France and Italy. They also stretch east through Italy, Switzerland, Germany, and Austria. Bordering Switzerland and Italy, the Matterhorn mountain attracts thousands of travelers for climbing and for its lovely views. Still, though surrounded by a heavily populated Europe, the Alps are far from tame. Hot winds sometimes blow, causing a sudden warming that can launch dangerous avalanches.

19

Formed by glaciers, the slopes leading up to the jagged peaks are covered with beech, oak, pine, and spruce. These forests are home to peregrine falcons nesting on high, rocky crags, swooping down to catch small birds in mid-flight.

Peregrine falcon

Beech

Chamois

Groups of nimble goatlike chamois leap from rocky ledge to ledge. Here they can graze on lichens and grasses. Even pine needles are edible food. As winter approaches, the chamois move down into the forested slopes.

The ibex lives even higher up on the Alps' snowline. A wild goat, the ibex has been heavily hunted for meat until it has become endangered. In the spring and summer, high mountain slopes bloom with mountain azalea, campanulas, and many other wildflowers. Golden eagles soar, hunting for rodents or even a chamois fawn.

Golden eagle

Ibex

Mountain azalea

The Himalayas

The Himalayas are the highest mountains in the world and they continue to grow. They are actually made up of several ranges running next to each other stretching 1,500 miles across southern Asia. The highest mountain in the world, Mt. Everest, stands between Tibet and Nepal at 29,028 feet. But one of the most spectacular mountains to view is the Annapurna.

The Himalayas rise from a tropical base. As they do so, the landscape changes. Their summits form a great barrier running roughly east to west. The dry uplands spread north in Tibet. The most eastern Himalayas are mountains of Szechwan. On the lower slopes their bamboo forests are home to the giant panda, another species in decline.

Giant panda

Bamboo

Rhododendron

Lesser panda

Up higher, dense rhododendron thickets hide the lesser panda.
Curled up to sleep during the day, the lesser panda descends at night
to eat bamboo, grasses, and small animals.

Still higher are scrubby spruce and pine. Here small groups of takin browse. At the highest point between the timberline and snowfields, bharal or "blue sheep" graze on open rocky slopes. Their blue-gray color hides them on the rocky hillsides of shale.

Bharal (blue sheep)

Takin

Tahr

Rhododendron

Yak

Dwarf rhododendrons grow on the rocky slopes of the Tibetan plateau. Farther north, the vegetation is more meager with sparse Himalayan birch and pine. Huge yaks and tahr travel in herds searching for food. Tibetan gazelles also graze here.

In the high mountains of Nepal, the elusive snow leopard hunts blue sheep. The snow leopard blends so well with its surroundings and is so secretive that it is rarely seen by humans. Still, it is hunted eagerly for its soft, silken coat. No one knows exactly how many snow leopards are really left, but it is hoped that their isolation will help to preserve this beautiful, endangered animal.

Though the Himalayas are remote and difficult to get to, many people still come to trek or climb these spectacular mountains. The sherpa—people who live here and work as farmers and porters—carry the baggage of climbers up the great peaks. Many visitors, as well as local inhabitants, have caused a critical loss of trees, which are cut down and used for firewood.

Snow leopard

Mountains Today

Despite their steep slopes and the severe climate, mountains are still vulnerable. The growing demand for country homes, mineral exploration, and old growth timber harvesting has threatened many mountain habitats throughout the world. Though many mountain ranges are included in protected parks now, they still suffer from overuse. Many parks have begun to develop permit systems to regulate the flow of recreation in mountain areas. They may seem indestructible, but the world's mountain habitats need to be protected from too much traffic and careless human use.

Glossary

alpine: relating to upland mountains, slopes

avalanche: a mass of snow, ice, or rock sliding down a mountain

burrow: a hole in the ground made by an animal as a den

continental divide: a mountain range that divides river systems flowing to opposite sides of a continent

elevation: the height to which something is raised

fault: a weakness or fracture in the Earth's crust

foothill: a hill at the foot of higher hills or mountains

forage: food for animals or the collection of food

glacier: a large body of ice moving slowly down a slope or outward from a central mass

gorge: a narrow ravine

habitat: a place where a plant or animal is naturally found

meadow: a tract of moist grassland

overgraze: to overfeed on a pasture, depleting its grassy cover

plateau: a large, level area raised above the surrounding land

plate: a huge, mobile segment of the Earth's crust

predator: an animal that lives by killing and consuming other animals

rodent: any of a large group of small mammals with sharp front teeth used for gnawing

shale: a rock made up of fine layers and formed from clay, mud, or silt

snow line: the elevation where the snow begins

tropical: relating to the tropics, where it is very hot and humid

upland: high land between the plains and mountains

Animals Index

Andean condor   18

Bald eagle   12

Bharal (blue sheep)   26

Bighorn sheep   12

Bison   9

Bobcat   7

Chamois   21, 22

Chinchilla   16

Cock-of-the-rock   18

Cougar   7, 8, 11

Coyote   11

Darwin's rhea   18

Deer   7, 13

Elk   9, 13

Giant panda   24

Golden eagle   22

Grizzly bear   8, 11

Grouse   7

Ibex   22

Lesser panda   25

Lynx   7

Marmot   12

Mice   7, 11

Mink   11

Mountain goat   12

Mule deer   10

Peregrine falcon   20

Pine marten   11

Ruffed grouse   10

Snow leopard   28

Snowshoe hare   7

Tahr   27

Takin   26

Tibetan gazelle   27

Vicuna   16, 17

Weasel   11

Whitetail deer   7

Yak   27

Plants Index

Alder   10

Balsamroot   13

Bamboo   24, 25

Bear grass   13

Beech   20

Bitterroot   13

Campanula   22

Chokecherry   10

Engelmann spruce   10

Himalayan birch   27

Indian paintbrush   13

Lichen   21

Lupine   13

Maple   10

Mountain azalea   22

Oak   20

Pine   20, 26, 27

Ponderosa pine   10

Rhododendron   25, 27

Spruce   20, 26

Water birch   10

Western larch   10

Wildflower   13

Wild geranium   13